Pepperoni Macaroni

Story by Alfred M. Struthers

Illustrations by Cathy Provoda

PEAR TREE PUBLISHING

Pepperoni Macaroni

Published by Pear Tree Publishing
www.PearTreePublishing.net

First Edition

Published in the United States of America

Struthers, Alfred M.
    Pepperoni Macaroni / by Alfred M. Struthers – 1st Ed.
    ISBN 978-1-62502-042-0
    Library of Congress Control Number: 2020923263

    1. Children's Book - Author. 2. Children's Book – Cooking. 3. Children's Book – Food
    I. Title II. Children's Book. III. Cooking

Cover & Book Design by Alfred M. Struthers and Cathy Provoda
Recipe courtesy of Joan Watson

1 2 3 4 5 6 7 8 9 10

Also by Alfred M. Struthers and Cathy Provoda
Did You Hear That?

For
Riley Marie Struthers

When Joni's parents
had a party,

they hired a fancy chef
named Marty.

Marty cleaned the countertop,

Then began to CHOP, CHOP, CHOP!

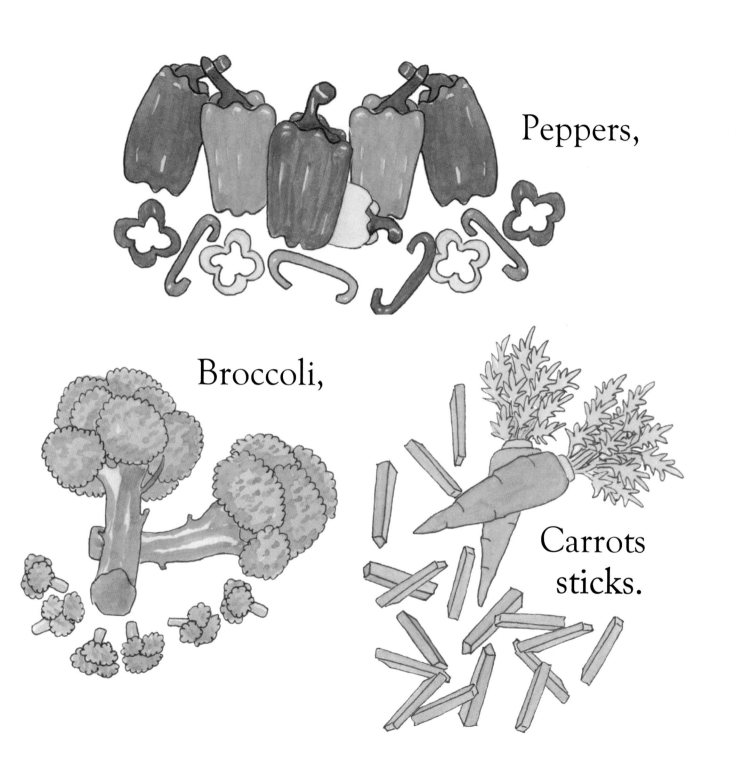

Peppers,

Broccoli,

Carrots
sticks.

Cantaloupe on red toothpicks!

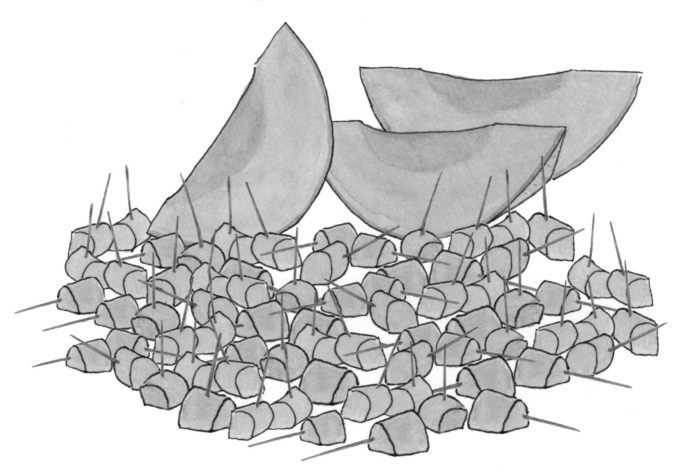

Joni didn't like the cooking.

She switched it all with no one looking.

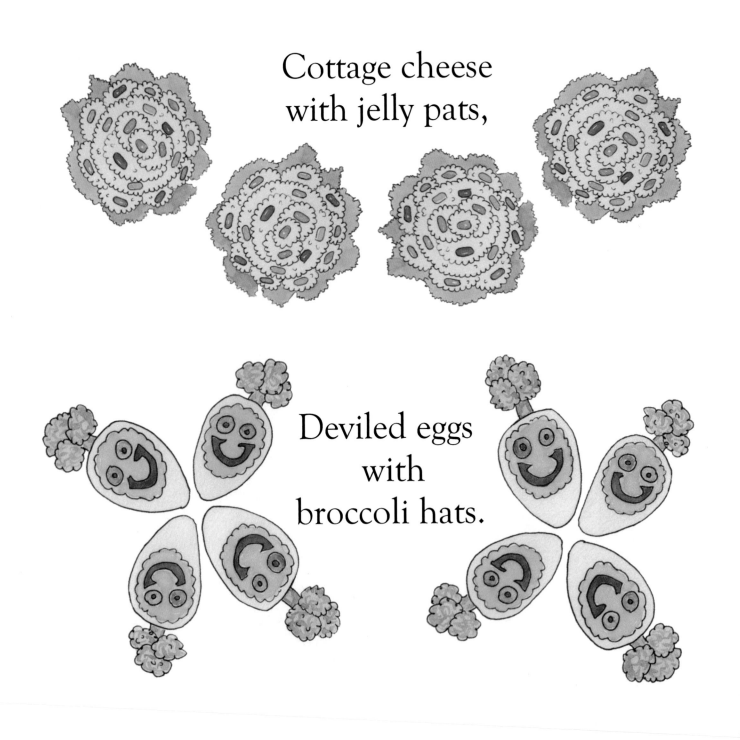

Cottage cheese
with jelly pats,

Deviled eggs
with
broccoli hats.

Apple slices topped with feta,

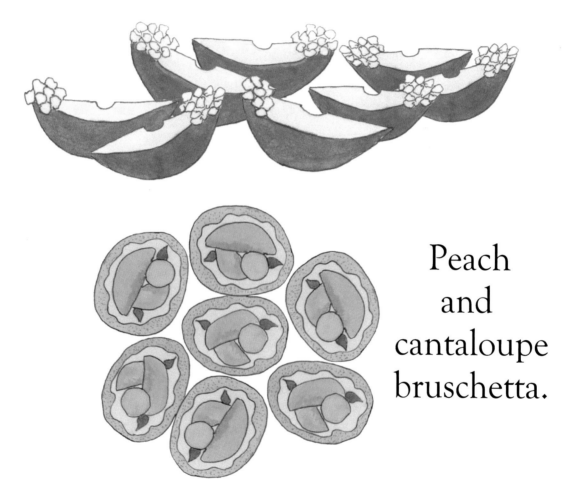

Peach
and
cantaloupe
bruschetta.

Few had seen such food before.
They ate it all and begged for more!

When Joni's Dad turned 52,
Uncle Frank made barbeque.

Lots of friends came by to eat.

Frank cooked seven kinds of meat.

Hot dogs,

Burgers,

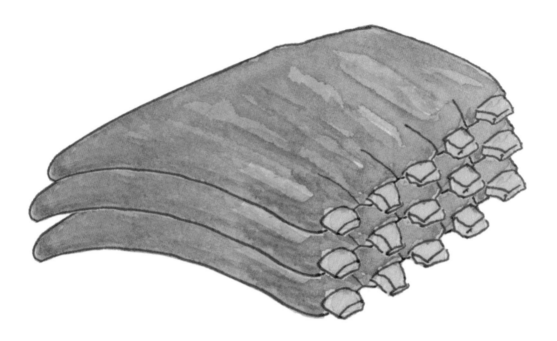

Ribs and Steak.

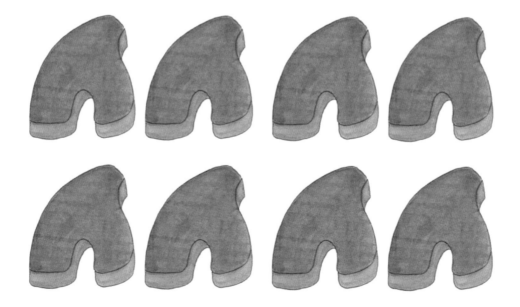

Chicken,

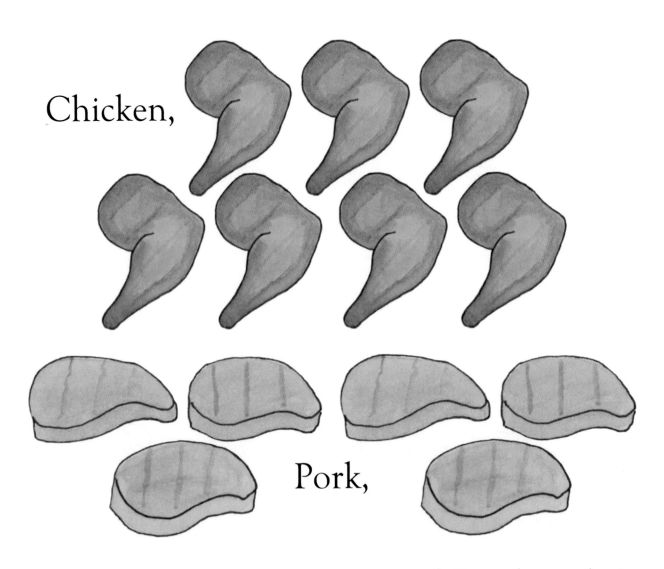

Pork,

...and Rattlesnake!

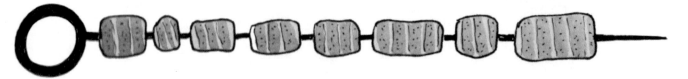

All that meat made Joni wince.

She dressed it up with condiments.

Pickle
skewers,

Mustard steaks,

Pork with red hot
pepper flakes.

Ginger chicken
wrapped in foil,

Steak tips
brushed with garlic oil.

It looked so good no one refused.
Uncle Frank was quite confused.

When Joni's cousin came to stay,
they had a Mexican buffet.

The chef
tied up
his apron
strings,
and
cooked
all kinds
of
spicy things.

Enchiladas,

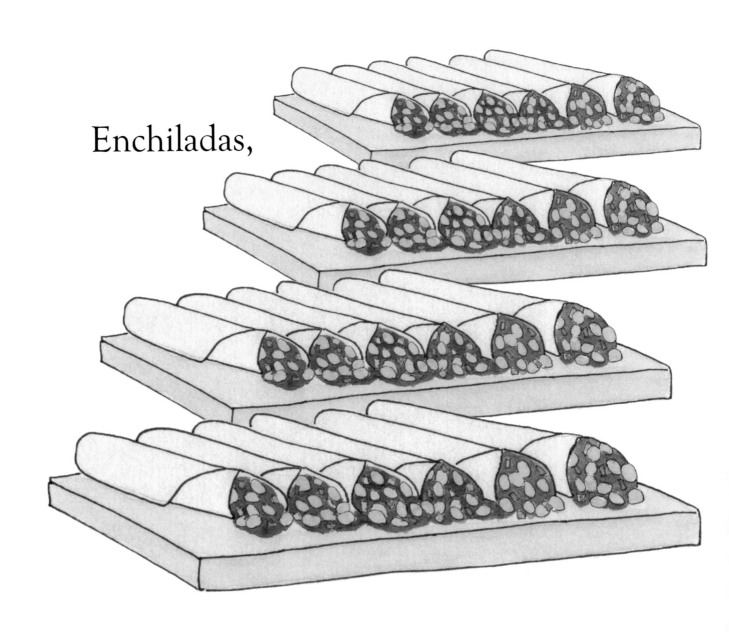

Beans and rice,

Jalapeños by the slice!

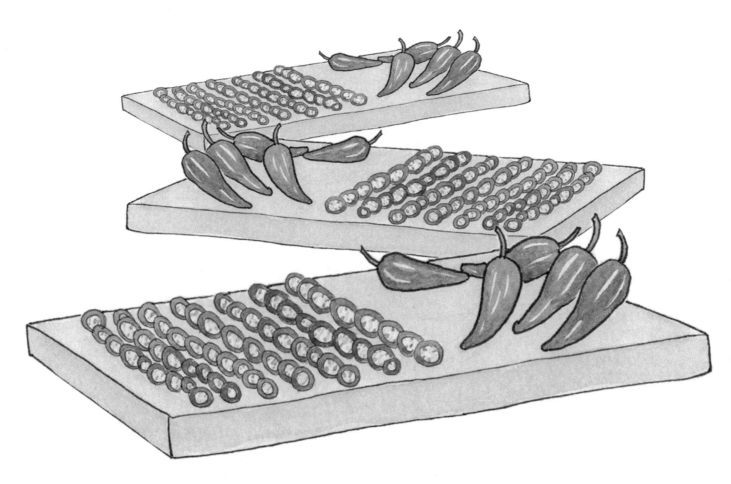

Joni had some reservations.

She made different combinations.

Cornbread wedges
filled with brie,

Refried beans
with sesame.

Braised beef tacos,

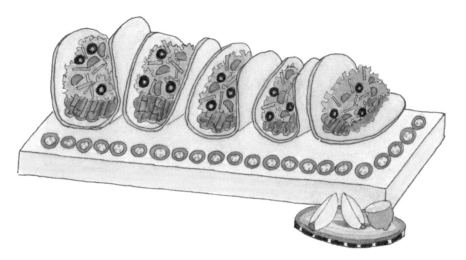

Spinach Rolls,

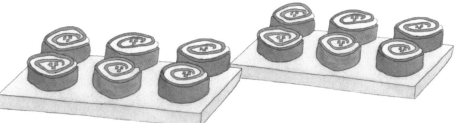

Mac and cheese tortilla bowls!

The chef knew something wasn't right,
but people raved to his delight.

Monday was the poker game.
The men got take-out just the same.

Find the menu. Contemplate.
Call it in, then sit and wait.

Chicken,

Pizza,

Chips and fries.

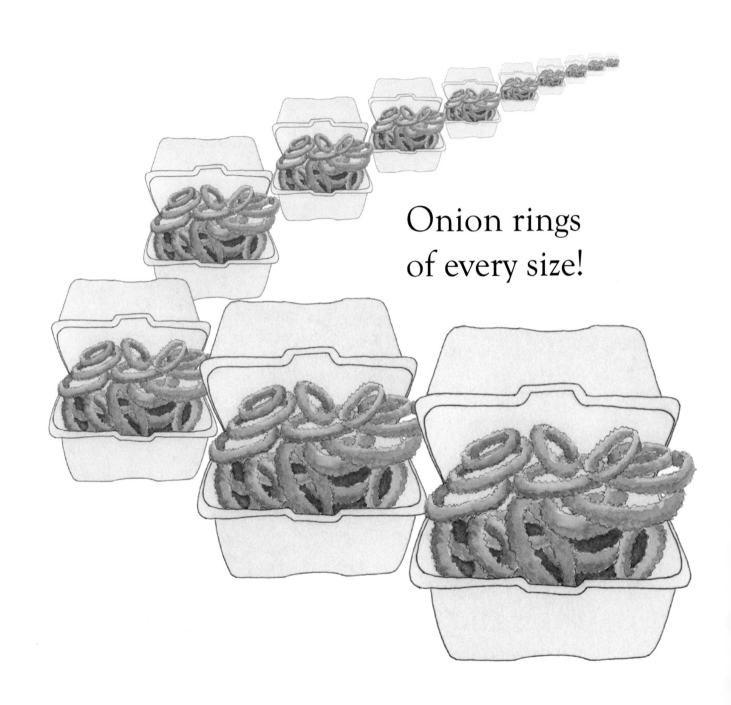

Onion rings
of every size!

It really didn't look that fit.

So, Joni spiced it up a bit.

Peanut butter
chicken strips,

Cheddar
cheese
with
parsley snips.

Pepper jelly chicken wraps,

Fries with honey mustard caps.

To some it seemed like just a blunder,
but Joni's dad began to wonder.

On Thursday, friends stopped by for bridge.

The grocer came and filled the fridge.

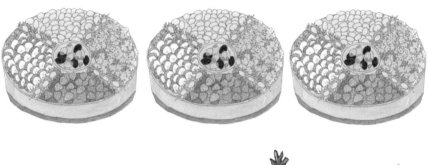

Three small platters,

One big plate,

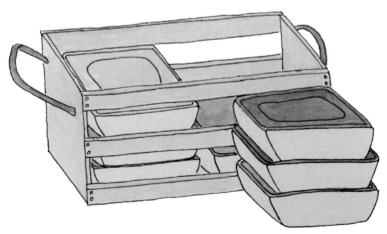

Seven dishes in a crate!

Dip with crackers,

Chunks of cheese,

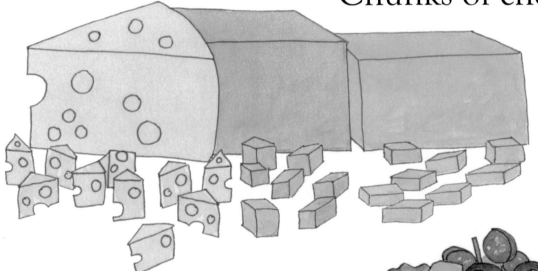

Chicken fingers
Cantonese.

Joni felt the need for change,

then began to rearrange.

Carrot strips with lemon glaze,

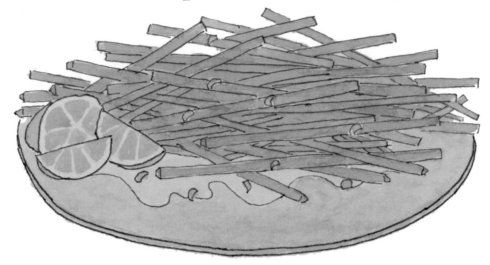

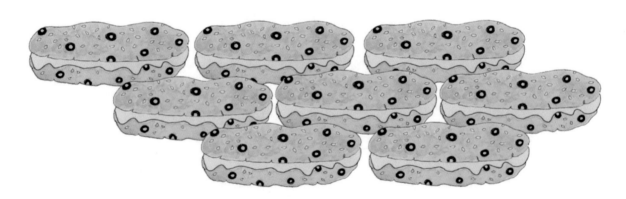

Olive bread with mayonnaise.

Broccoli slaw on Melba toast,

Mushrooms stuffed with artichokes!

The friends said, "This is quite delicious!"
Joni's Mom became suspicious.

On Joni's graduation day,
they hired the pastry chef, René.

He wore
a big white
fluffy hat,
rattled pans
and scared the cat!

Caramel cookies,

Lemon
Tarts,

Frosted muffins,

Candy hearts.

After much consideration,

Joni made an alteration.

First the cookies, then the crepes...

But wait!

Who's that
behind
the drapes?

While all the other people snacked,
Mom caught Joni in the act!

Now the question Joni had:
would her parents *both* be mad?

Would they yell and would they curse?
Or would her punishment be even worse?

No more phone,

and no TV?

Doing housework constantly?

Washing dishes?

Cleaning floors?

Doing all the rubbish chores?

It took some time for them to choose.

Then they came and broke the news.

And when she heard what they'd selected,

it wasn't quite what she expected.

They threw a bash by invitation.

The summer's biggest celebration.

Lots of tables,

lots of chairs,

Tiki torches on the stairs.

Many things
to set
the mood,
but this time
Joni
made the food!

Her parents thought it only fitting.

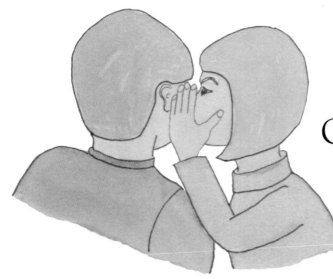

One guest whispered,
"are you kidding?"

But everyone was quite impressed.

And guess which dish they loved the best?

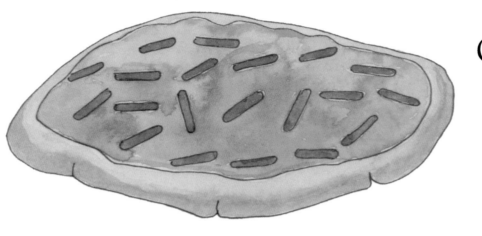

Green Bean
Pizza?

Almond Stars?

Chunky Chocolate
Raisin Bars?

Peanut Noodles?

Popcorn Rice?

Bubblegum Italian Ice?

Razzle Dazzle
Ice Cream Pie?

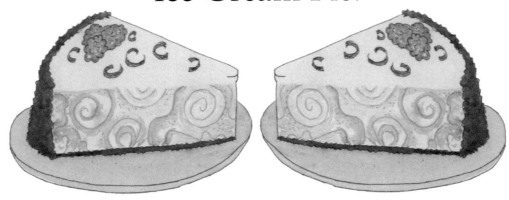

Applesauce on
marbled rye?

The favorite entrée made by Joni was...

Pepperoni Macaroni!

The End

Joni's Recipes

English Muffin Pizza

1. Split and toast the muffins. Place cut side up on baking sheet.

2. Add a slice of mozzarella cheese. Putting cheese down before sauce keeps the muffin from getting soggy.

3. Spread a spoon of spaghetti sauce on top of cheese.

4. Top with cooked sausage, pepperoni, bacon or any topping you like.

5. Add a sprinkle of oregano or Italian seasoning.

6. Bake at 350 degrees until cheese is melted and gooey.

About the Author

Alfred M. Struthers lives in Peterborough, New Hampshire. In addition to crafting books that inspire, entertain and make a difference in the lives of young readers, Mr. Struthers is a singer/songwriter, furniture maker, and avid collector of fossils that line the streambeds around Cooperstown, New York. In addition to *Pepperoni Macaroni*, he has published *Did You Hear That?* (illustrated by Cathy Provoda), and five books in the Third Floor Mystery Series, including: *The Case of Secrets, The Phantom Vale, The Curse of Halim, The Demon Tide,* and *The Stone Ghost.*

About the Illustrator

Cathy Provoda lives in Peterborough NH with her partner Richard. When not painting, she can be found in her gardens or playing bluegrass music on her autoharp. She is the founder of Blueberry Cove Creations where her artwork is displayed (blueberrycovecreations.com), including wildlife note cards, chicken-centric greeting cards, and her first illustrated book collaboration, *Did You Hear That? Pepperoni Macaroni* is her second book collaboration. Joni's cat was inspired by "Snickers"—beloved pet of Cathy's longtime friend, Ellen.

Recipe provided by Joan's Personal Chef Service

A former elementary school teacher, Joan Watson is a New Hampshire native who loves creating meals for kids and grown-ups alike. Learn more about her at www.chefjoan.com

Made in the USA
Middletown, DE
05 September 2022

73270426R00035